A LITTLE BIT OF MISCHIEF

For Daisy, Tove and Catrin with love from Granny;
Kieran, Izabelle and Cassidy with love from Grannyjen ~ J.S.

For Joseff, Jacob, and every other mischievous child ~ G.H.

First published in 2010 by Pont Books, an imprint of
Gomer Press, Llandysul, Ceredigion, SA44 4JL

ISBN 978 1 84851 047 0
A CIP record for this title is available from the British Library.

This book is published with the financial support
of the Welsh Books Council.

Printed and bound in Wales at
Gomer Press, Llandysul, Ceredigion

A LITTLE BIT OF MISCHIEF

Jenny Sullivan · Graham Howells

Pont

Mum didn't notice Cari's thundercloud as she helped her get ready for school.

Huuuumph! thought Cari crossly. *I don't get a choice.*

Inside Techniquest, Mr Lavery spoke sternly. 'You can go anywhere you like, but remember – everyone will know you're from Ysgol y Cwm!'

'I'll push you,' said Nia.

'No thanks,' said Cari, her thundercloud growing bigger and blacker.

'Come with us,' said Billy.

'Can't,' said Cari and watched her friends scatter
everywhere, pushing levers, splashing water, shouting.

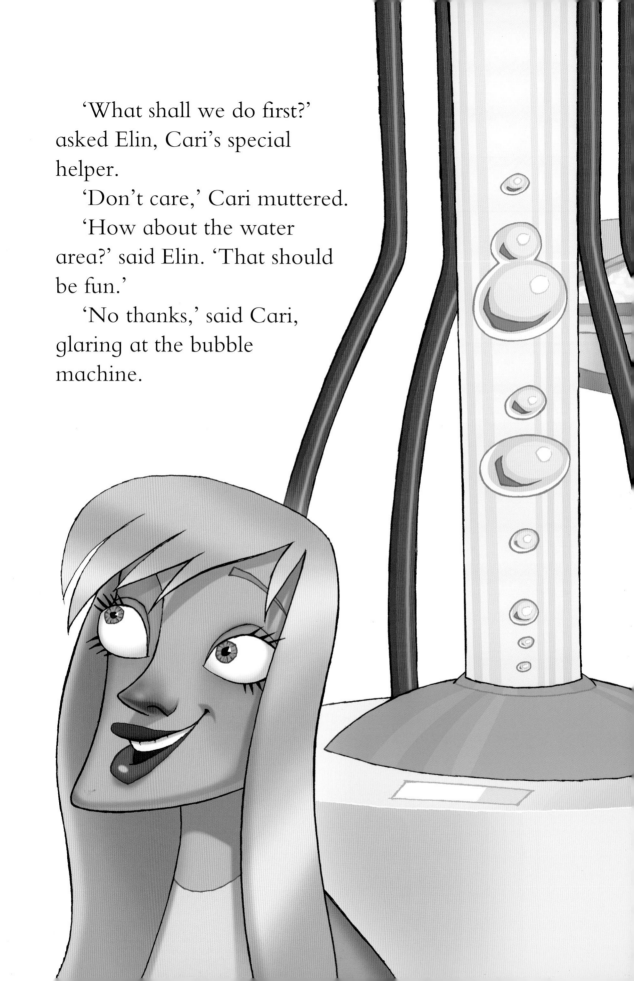

'What shall we do first?' asked Elin, Cari's special helper.

'Don't care,' Cari muttered.

'How about the water area?' said Elin. 'That should be fun.'

'No thanks,' said Cari, glaring at the bubble machine.

'Bullies!' she said. 'The big bubbles are eating the little ones.'

'I wonder what this is?' said Elin, wetting her hands and rubbing the handles.

The bowl made a strange sound and then, like magic, began to spout water!

'You have a go!' said Elin.

'No point,' Cari grumped. 'I know what it does, now.'

Next Elin found a huge balloon. 'Let me see,' she said. 'You press this button until it's hot enough for lift-off. That sounds like fun, doesn't it, Cari?'

Elin bent over the machine. 'If I just sit here,' she said, 'maybe we can . . .'

But Cari had other ideas. First she found a huge ball full of coloured liquid.

She spun the rim and the ball slowly started to move. 'Magic!' said Cari.

Then she spotted a really good place to hide . . .

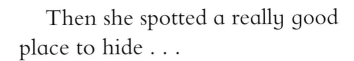

In the darkness, everything glowed and gleamed.
Inside the sphere there was a silent thunderstorm.
Cari flattened her hand against the glass.
The lightning made her jump. That was fun!
She did it again, and again. Amazing!
Then she heard Elin's voice outside. 'Cari?
Where are you?' Elin sounded cross.

'Cari? Has anyone seen Cari?'
Oh dear, thought Cari. *I hope she doesn't find me.*

Then a bright flash startled her and made her blink.

Cari wheeled her chair round. How weird! She could see her shadow on the screen.

That was great, she thought. *Where can I go next?*

Cari wheeled herself to the lift and waited till some people got out.

As she sailed up, she could see all her friends below. *This is AWESOME!* she thought.

She rode up-and-down-and-up in the lift four times.

Upstairs, she whizzed across the piano keys and played a jangly tune with her wheels.

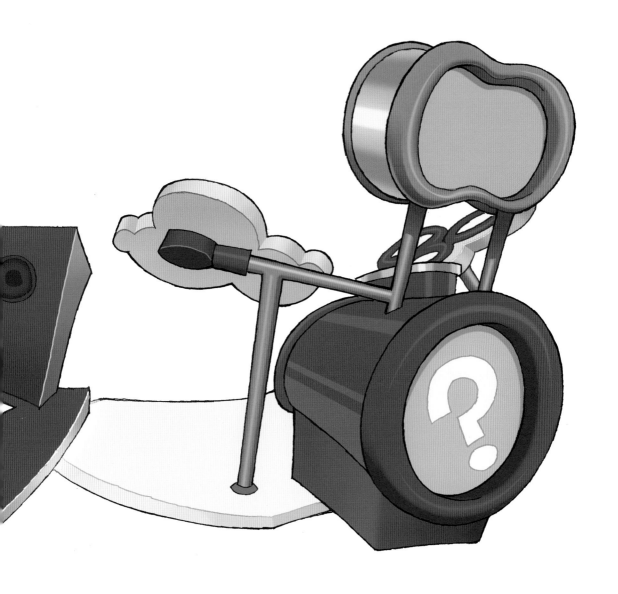

She bashed the drums, and waved her hand at a metal pole. It made an amazing, screechy wail.

Wow! This is cool, thought Cari. Her big black cloud had almost disappeared.

But then she saw something that made her change her mind . . .

'Fooled you!' shouted Darren. 'You thought my head was cut off, didn't you?'

'Just for a minute,' said Cari.

'It's only mirrors,' said Darren. 'Hey, d'you know everyone's looking for you?'

Cari giggled.

Darren grinned. 'What shall we do now?'

'Go and hide in the dark room?' suggested Cari.

On the way to the lift Darren pushed Cari's chair fast and made her shriek.

When they rode in the lift,
no one saw them.

They found a big hollow tube in the corner and
shouted into it. 'Yoooooo-hoooooo!'
The tube echoed back. '*Yooooooooo-hooooooooo-oooo!*'

Everybody heard the yoo-hoo-hooing . . .
even the grown-ups.

'There you are, you naughty girl!'
yelled Elin. 'I've been so worried!'

Mr Lavery spoke sternly. 'Cari,' he said. 'We've all been looking for you. I didn't think *you*'d be naughty!' Cari beamed. 'It was just a little bit of mischief,' she said. Her big, black thundercloud had gone.

'Did you have a good time today, sweetheart?'
Mum asked as she tucked Cari up in bed that night.
'Best ever,' Cari sighed. 'And I did it all by myself.'

ABOUT TECHNIQUEST

Cari's visit to Techniquest is imaginary, but thousands of children every year visit this ground-breaking discovery centre in the heart of Cardiff Bay.

Founded in 1985, Techniquest has long outgrown its original premises, moving to the UK's first purpose-built Science Centre in 1995. It welcomes visitors of all kinds: individuals, families and organised groups are able to enjoy more than 120 different activities and hands-on exhibits.

Before her visit, Cari imagines that she is not going to be able to do things for herself, but the key to Techniquest's success is its accessibility to all. There is easy wheelchair access, including a lift, to all parts of the building and visitors are encouraged to try out all the activities for themselves. Staff are always on hand to help, if needed. Independent exploration is all-important and, as Cari discovers, there are very few boundaries in this safe and secure environment.

A visit to Techniquest can be a mind-changing experience even when, like Cari, you learn less about technology and more about yourself and your own potential.

Author Jenny Sullivan and illustrator Graham Howells thoroughly enjoyed their research at Techniquest and we at Gomer Press would like to thank the centre for their help and hospitality.

Why not find out more about Techniquest? You can do so by visiting:

www.techniquest.org